Arabella's Web

by Enid Richemont

Illustrated by Gabriele Antonini

FRANKLIN WATTS
LONDON•SYDNEY

First published in 2015 by
Franklin Watts
338 Euston Road
London
NW1 3BH

Franklin Watts Australia
Level 17/207 Kent Street
Sydney
NSW 2000

A CIP catalogue record for this book is available
from the British Library.

ISBN 978 1 4451 3774 2 (hbk)
ISBN 978 1 4451 3777 3 (pbk)
ISBN 978 1 4451 3776 6 (library ebook)
ISBN 978 1 4451 3775 9 (ebook)

Series Editor: Jackie Hamley
Series Advisor: Catherine Glavina
Series Designer: Peter Scoulding

Printed in China

Franklin Watts is a division of
Hachette Children's Books,
an Hachette UK company.
www.hachette.co.uk

For David Richemont,
star-gazer – E.R.

Arabella Spider was
trying to spin a web.

She tried across the window. Oh dear!

She tried across
Danny's bike.

Oh dear! Oh dear!

Arabella tried the plum tree.

Then Dad picked
the plums.

She tried Gran's new straw hat.

"Aaagh! A spider!"
yelled Gran.

13

She tried the bushes.

Then it rained.

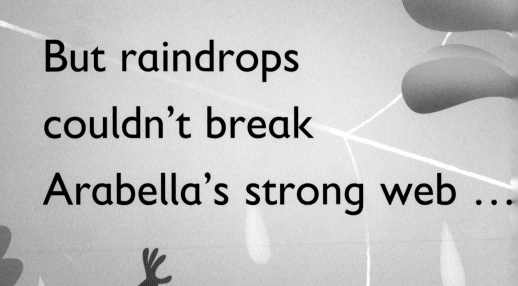

But raindrops
couldn't break
Arabella's strong web ...

16

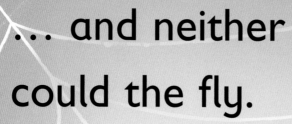

... and neither
could the fly.

"Dinner, yummy yummy!" thought Arabella Spider.

Puzzle Time!

Put these pictures in the right order and tell the story!

cross

pleased

angry

happy

Which words describe Arabella in the top picture? Which describe her in the bottom picture?

Turn over for answers!

Notes for adults

TADPOLES are structured to provide support for newly independent readers. The stories may also be used by adults for sharing with young children.

Starting to read alone can be daunting. **TADPOLES** help by providing visual support and repeating words and phrases. These books will both develop confidence and encourage reading and rereading for pleasure.

If you are reading this book with a child, here are a few suggestions:

1. Make reading fun! Choose a time to read when you and the child are relaxed and have time to share the story.
2. Talk about the story before you start reading. Look at the cover and the blurb. What might the story be about? Why might the child like it?
3. Encourage the child to employ a phonics first approach to tackling new words by sounding the words out.
4. Invite the child to retell the story, using the jumbled picture puzzle as a starting point. Extend vocabulary with the matching words to pictures puzzle.
5. Give praise! Remember that small mistakes need not always be corrected.

Answers

Here is the correct order:

1.e 2.b 3.d 4.a 5.f 6.c

Words to describe Arabella in the top picture: angry, cross

Words to describe her in the bottom picture: happy, pleased